Freddie and Millie

Go to the Seaside

Written by Caroline Farnham

Illustrated by Carolina Rico

Grosvenor House
Publishing Limited

This book is published by
Grosvenor House Publishing Ltd
Link House
140 The Broadway, Tolworth, Surrey, KT6 7HT.
www.grosvenorhousepublishing.co.uk

This book is a work of fiction. Any resemblance to
people or events, past or present, is purely coincidental.

A CIP record for this book
is available from the British Library

ISBN 978-1-80381-036-2
eBook ISBN 978-1-80381-179-6

For Isabelle Grace x

Best Wishes
Caroline Farnham
x

Here is a story about two cheeky rabbits,
Both of whom have some very naughty habits.
One is called Freddie, the other is called Millie,
Both you will find, behave very silly.

Freddie is a boy, he's big and white,
Millie a girl, with grey and white stripes.
Both have floppy ears that are really rather big,
And large fluffy feet to help them to dig.

Izzy is a girl who looks after them well,
She feeds them, cuddles them and keeps them
looking swell.

Now that you know how these bunnies look,
It's time to turn the page on this rabbit story book.

WAIT! Before you start there is one thing you must do.
Make yourself look like them, yes that means you!
Wriggle your nose and make ears like a bunny.
Look in the mirror, don't you look funny!
You're definitely a rabbit that's for sure!
So, turn the page for the rabbit adventure.

It's an exciting day for Millie and Freddie,
They've packed a bag and brought along teddy.
They're off to the seaside! Oh, what fun,
They're hoping to see sand, sea and sun.

7

Hopping on a train with Izzy to the coast,
"We're off to the sea," they exclaim, "it's
what we love most."
As they sit on the train, with the world flashing by,
They chitter chatter and excitedly cry,
"Let's get a bucket and spade and build a castle from sand,
And build a moat around it to keep others off our land!"

Once they arrive, they dash from the train,
Hoping that the sun keeps away the rain.
"Let's get to the beach, it's our favourite place,
As fast as we can, let's have a race!"

Out of breath they arrive on the sand,
Bucket and spade and ice cream in hand.
"Let's build a sandcastle high into the sky,
And surround it with sea water for the boats to go by."

So off they hop to the sea with a jig,
"Be careful bunnies, those waves are big."
Then out of nowhere, a wave hits like thunder,
Throwing Freddie in the air and dragging him under.

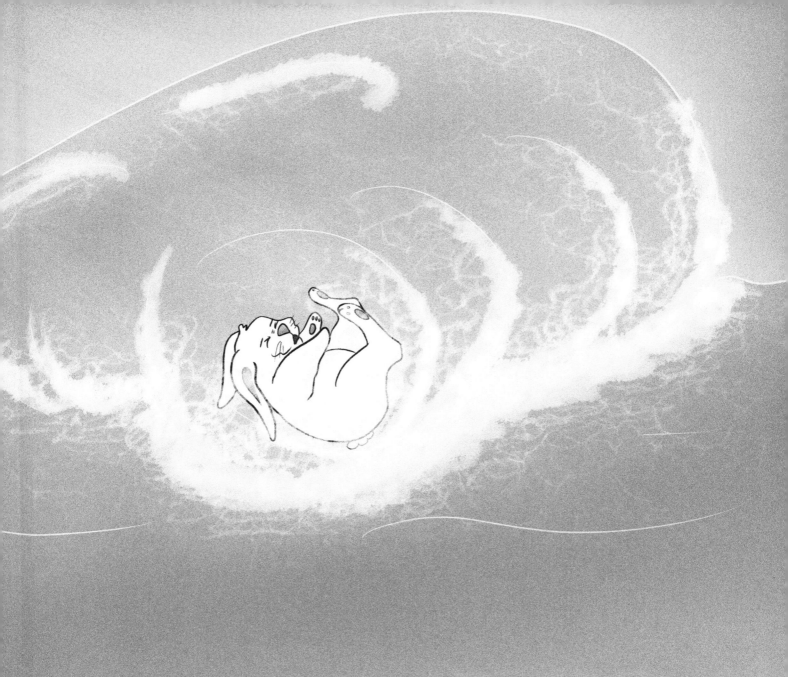

"Help, help, help!" Millie did shout,
"The wave has Freddie and it's dragging him out."
Quick as a flash Izzy ran to the sea,
Grabbing Freddie as fast as could be...

Coughing and spluttering back on the shore,
"Are you ok Freddie? You look awfully poor."
"I didn't see it coming, I went in too deep,
The wave came from nowhere and knocked me off my feet!"

"You're very lucky this time, but you need to think,
The sea is dangerous and you can easily sink!
Let's get back on the sand and stay by the shore."
"I promise I won't go in too deep anymore."

"I'm glad we're on land and away from the sea,
I like playing in the sand, it's much safer for me!"
Izzy got them an ice cream to make them feel better,
Then the rain came and made Freddie even wetter!

Lightning Source UK Ltd.
Milton Keynes UK
UKHW050902250722
406322UK00005B/71